46

  **three Billy-goats Gruff**

 **flowers**

 **nest**

 **grass**

 **herbs**

 **river**

 **meadow**

 **water**

 **bridge**

These pictures are some of the characters and things the story tells about. Let the child to whom you are reading SEE and SAY them.

Then, as you read the story text and come to a picture instead of a word, pause and point to the picture for your listener to SEE and SAY.

You'll be amazed at how quickly children catch on and enjoy participating in the story telling.

 big Billy-goat Gruff

 second Billy-goat Gruff

ISBN 0-86163-810-7
Copyright © 1984 Award Publications Limited
This edition first published 1995
Second impression 1997
Published by Award Publications Limited,
27 Longford Street, London NW1 3DZ
Printed in Belgium

young Billy-goat Gruff

 **Troll**

 **hooves**

 **houses**

 **horns**

 **cakes**

The Story of the
Three Billy Goats Gruff

AWARD PUBLICATIONS LIMITED

There were once **3** goats who lived among high hills, where wild  grew and eagles had their . The **3** goats were brothers and their family name was Gruff.

The roamed among the hills each day searching for sweet and to eat. And one day they came to a deep . On the far side they could see a full of long juicy . "The is very deep but there is a ," said . "We must cross that."

 said he would like to cross the  first. So trip, trap, trip, trap went his  as he ran on to the wooden  .

Now under this there lived

a who was very nasty. A

is a big, bad goblin and this one

was very big and bad indeed.

Whenever he heard steps on the

he shouted, "Keep away or

I'll gobble you up!" So no one had

tried to cross the for years.

But now, here was  happily trip, trapping across the . As soon as the  heard him he shouted, "I'll gobble you up."

 was very frightened by the  but he said in a small voice, "Please let me cross the . My brother  is coming soon. He's much fatter than I."

So the greedy let cross over the to the beyond.

People who lived in the on the hills above were amazed. It was their . They had built it. But no one had crossed it since the came to live beneath it.

No one had dared to cross the  since then. were warned, "Don't cross it to fly your on the hills beyond the ."

The  werc told, "Don't cross the  to gather  in the . Keep away from the ."

So of course everyone was very surprised

to see  trotting over the  .

Then as soon as he reached the  ,

along came  . Trip, trap, trip, trap

went his  as he ran onto the

wooden  . "Keep off!" shouted

the  , "or I'll gobble you up."

He looked so ugly  almost ran away.

But no, he stood firmly on the  instead and spoke softly to the . "Please don't gobble me up. will be coming soon. There is more of him to eat."

So the greedily said once more, "All right. I'll wait." And crossed to the and went skipping away with his little brother.

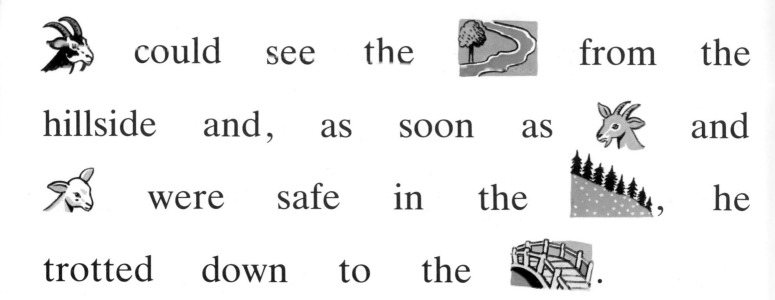 could see the 🌳 from the hillside and, as soon as 🐐 and 🐑 were safe in the 🌲, he trotted down to the 🌉.

Trip, trap, trip, trap, went his  as he ran on to the ![bridge]. When the ![troll] saw him he shouted, "I'm going to gobble you up."

 snorted and stamped and bellowed, "You just try!" Then he lowered his  and Thump! He butted the  right off the .

Away went the  falling down, down to the . He disappeared into the deep and no one ever saw him again.

and were jumping for joy in the . They ran down to meet as he trotted over the . "We knew you could beat that ," they said.

Then the people came out of the  on the hills and ran to the  too. They could cross the  as much as they liked now. There was no horrid  to stop them. They brought honey for  to eat, and gave them juicy and little cream cheeses.

The  and came to the and made chains of for , and everyone was happy.

Now  could cross the to fly their and could pick whenever they liked in the , where stayed and made their home.